CW01021847

To Geoff & Jean,
Thank you for your help
with the computer
Best wishes
Christine     cald'Albert
HFoxall

# Lawley and the

# Magical Legends of Shropshire

Christine M. d'Albert

*Illustrated by Helen Foxall*

YOUCAXTON PUBLICATIONS

OXFORD & SHREWSBURY

FOR MY THREE DAUGHTERS
AND MY GRANDSONS CAMERON AND LUKE

# CONTENTS

| | |
|---|---|
| LAWLEY | 1 |
| FLYING FLAGS | 6 |
| GRANPA CARADOC | 10 |
| DRAGON MAGIC AT STIPERSTONES | 16 |
| SHREWSBURY SHOEMAKER | 23 |
| HARVEST AT LEEBOTWOOD | 30 |
| SH! IPPIKIN WILL CATCH YOU | 38 |
| GRAN'S SECRET | 45 |
| WHERE ARE THE MATCHES? | 51 |
| MITCHELL THE WITCH | 59 |
| MISCHIEF IN SHREWSBURY | 65 |
| STOKESAY GIANTS' TREASURE | 73 |
| MAP | 82 |

# *LAWLEY*

Deep down in the darkness of the earth, the rumbling began. A little lizard dragon woke up. He felt a tickling then a wriggling in the rocks around him. It seemed as if giant hands were squeezing his body. Waves of sound battered him and he was smothered in smoke.

People were celebrating the New Year. The noise from their fireworks echoed in the earth below. This was the magic that woke the little lizard dragon. This is what he had been waiting for.

Pulling himself forwards like a worm he followed the sounds and slid his soft body into an underground pool. He giggled and blew streams of tiny bubbles.

Noticing a light shining above him, he squeezed himself through a hole like toothpaste from a tube and climbed upwards. He grew longer and thinner, then Pop. The little lizard dragon popped out into our world. Still the silver ball of light hung high above him. It was the moon.

At that same moment a young boy was peering out of his bedroom window. Sam was staying with his Gran and Gramps for the Christmas holidays.

Tonight he'd been allowed to stay up late to watch the fireworks. He was tired now but he just could not sleep.

As he stared into the darkness Sam noticed how the moonlight brushed the buckets, trees and the shed with silver. The garden looked magical. Up on the hillside he saw a plume of silvery smoke. Whatever could that be? He was too tired to think. It must be investigated tomorrow. He crawled into bed and went fast asleep.

Next morning Sam jumped out of bed and rushed downstairs.

'Gran, Dotty and I are going to play in the orchard.'

'Enjoy yourselves but put your gloves on, it's cold outside.'

With Gran's dog Dotty yapping at his heels, Sam ran up the garden and on up through the orchard. He swung round the trees singing his favourite songs as loud as he could. When he reached the pile of rocks in the steepest corner he flopped down. This was his secret place, where he played pirates, spacemen and explorers. Then he remembered the silvery plume of smoke he'd seen last night. He must search for clues.

Meanwhile, deep underground the little lizard dragon had lain in the pool all night long. The sound of Sam's singing woke him and he was curious. He slid out of the warm water and climbed up and up the slippery slope.

Suddenly everything went dark.

He heard panting and puffing and there was a strong smell of dog food and bones. Bump. His snout pushed into Dotty's wet nose, she fell backwards and knocked Sam over. There was a heap of boy, dog and a lizard dragon. Legs and arms were tangled in a huge wet tail. For a few seconds there was silence as they stared at one another. They were all a bit scared.

Sam spoke first, his voice wobbled a bit,

'Hallo, I'm Sam. Who are you?'

A loud voice boomed out, 'I'm Lawley, pleased to meet you.'

The lizard dragon looked down in dismay. Sam and Dotty lay on the ground covering their ears with hands and paws. Oh dear, what had he done? Sam explained that his voice was far too loud and asked if he would whisper instead.

'Sorry,' said Lawley, 'is this better?'

'Well a bit better, but your quietest of whispers would be just right.'

Lawley grinned. He was so pleased to have two new friends. Sam gently touched the lizard dragon's huge tail and asked him where he had come from.

'I'm Lawley the little lizard dragon and I love fire and fireworks. I was born hundreds of years ago in an exploding volcano. As it cooled it made this hill and I've lived inside it for years and years. I've been waiting to be woken up. You see every fifty years one of my tribe wakes up and comes into your world. Your fireworks woke me, now it's my turn to share time with you, Sam.'

Lawley explained how his Granpa Doc had cast a spell when he was very young.

Sam wanted to hear about it so Lawley whispered it

'Lawley, my little grandson.

When the earth rumbles

And tickles your tum,

Wriggle and squirm,

Change into a worm,

Little lizard dragon,

Make magic have fun.'

Sam chuckled, 'We'll have to change your name. You're not little any more, you're a Giant' and Sam started to sing.'Little Lawley's, getting talleee

Smallee Lawley, Now he's HUGE.'

Sam collapsed in a heap of giggles with his arms wrapped round Lawley's tail.

'Next time you look across from the village, you'll see my hill with my snout pointing to Shrewsbury and the tip of my tail tickling Granpa Doc's nose. So young friends here I am, Lawley the Giant Lizard Dragon at your service.' the huge creature bowed low in front of his friends.

Time had raced by and Sam heard Gran calling them back for lunch. They all agreed to meet again the next day.

Lawley was left on the pile of rocks, daydreaming. As the friends left, Sam looked back, blinked twice and Lawley was gone. Mm, magic he thought and smiled.

# *FLYING FLAGS*

'Come on Dotty, let's go and play'. Sam ran to the topmost part of the garden, climbed on to the pile of rocks and shouted, 'Lawleeeeee.'

The sound spiralled down deep into the earth, followed by silence... nothing, no-one answered. A faint gurgling began then.. Whoosh. Both were hit by a fountain of water and up popped Lawley with a big grin on his face.

'I've brought something to show you, Lawley.' said Sam, pulling a long stick wrapped in cloth from his pocket. Dotty ready for a game, grabbed one end in her teeth and pulled.

'No, Dotty, let go.' Luckily she opened her mouth to bark and the stick dropped to the ground. Sam unrolled the cloth it was a green and white flag with a red dragon in the middle.

Lawley smiled, 'I know some white dragons but not any red ones.'

'This is the red dragon of Wales,' Sam explained. 'We wave these at the Welsh Rugby matches and cheer. We ought to make one for you.'

'Yippee! I must have one long enough for my tail. I want a purple dragon flag. Let's start now.'

Sam thought hard. Gran had given him an old sheet to make a tent. That would do. A tall bean stick from Gramps' shed and maybe he'd find some paint there too.

'Just a minute Lawley, what happens if Gran or Gramps comes up here and sees you?'

Lawley laughed, 'Have you forgotten I'm magic? I'm covered in invisible powder so no-one can see me, except you and Dotty.'

Sam opened the shed door and rummaged around inside. He came out pulling the sheet like a snake behind him. Lawley grabbed one end and told the others to hold the rest tight, while he tore off a long piece, just the right size.

'My flag, here's my flag,' naughty lizard dragon shouted as he whirled the strip above his head. Sam caught the end and began drawing the creature's body in the middle. He hadn't heard Gramps come up the path.

'That's a big picture Sam. It's a bit long and thin though.'

'It's a flag for a Giant Dragon, it must be huge. I'm going to paint it purple.'

'Well I never,' said Gramps, 'let's see what colours I can find.' and would you believe it Gramps walked right through Lawley's tail. Thank goodness the magic worked.

'Here's some ink,' Gramps held two bottles covered in cobwebs. One label was Red and the other Blue. 'If you mix these together it should make bright purple.'

Sam began to paint, ink ran in trickling rivers of purple over the body. He dabbed on red toes and large blue spots on the tail. Gramps and Sam stood back to admire the work.'It looks more like a kite than a flag,' said Gramps. 'Try it, but tie a long string at one end or it'll fly away in this wind.' And off he went to do some more work in the garden.

Lawley held on to one corner while Sam held the string and Dotty held the other one. Wind tugged at the cloth, pulling it from Dotty and leaving Sam to hold the string very tightly. The wind took away Lawley's voice as he began to sing,

'I have a kite, it's purple and bright,
Flying high with clouds in the sky.
Like an aeroplane wing,
Dives, dips then swings
It's great, it's the best. Let it fly.'

Gramps looked up from his digging and thought Sam must be an expert kite-flyer to have launched it all on his own. But of course he couldn't see the lizard dragon helping him.

When the flying finished Sam rolled up the kite and gave it to Lawley.

'You keep it underground, it'll be safer there. We can fly it another day and cheer for you and your tribe.'

In a flash Lawley and his kite disappeared. Sam and Dotty jumped off the pile of rocks and ran down to ask Gran for a drink.

# *GRANPA CARADOC*

Sam rushed his breakfast and called Dotty and together they ran through the orchard to find Lawley. Soon the three friends were sitting on the hill looking down on Gramps in the garden.

'I have a grandfather,' said Lawley. 'I call him Doc for short, but his real name is Caradoc. Would you like to visit him?'

Sam was thinking hard. Lawley was old. His father would be much older. Lawley's grandfather must be very, very old.

'My grandfather is as old as the hills.' Lawley chuckled, 'In fact my grandfather lives in a hill. One day thousands of years ago a volcano exploded and

Granpa was born. Molten rock like hot chocolate sauce cooled into the shape of a hill and Granpa Doc has lived inside it ever since.'

'An exploding grandfather, wow' Sam was impressed.

'Granpa is the leader of our great Magma tribe. There are Wrekin, Ragleth and me,' said Lawley, 'and we all have trilobite badges.'

Sam's eyes sparkled, 'So Granpa Doc wasn't born, he just came up like a pimple.' Then he began to sing,

It's simple, it's simple
He started as a crinkle,
Then became a wrinkle
Next a huge, great pimple.
Up popped Doc
Inside a massive great rock.

The others joined in and marched around singing as loud as they could. What a noise. They were soon out of breath and flopped down in the grass.

'Come on, let's go and see Granpa Doc.' Lawley wrapped his scaly tail round Sam and Dotty and lifted them on to his back. 'All aboard the Lawley Express. Hold tight.'

Wings unfolded beneath Sam's feet. They creaked as Lawley took off. He flew down the valley and landed on a hillside near a cave. Sam and Dotty jumped down and followed the giant lizard dragon into a dark, damp cave. Sam was a bit frightened.

'Don't worry Sam, remember Granpa's magic will keep us from harm. Now we must find the secret passage.'

In the far corner a sliver of light shone through a crack. Sam held on to Lawley's tail and one by one they squeezed through into a dark passage. It was slippery in places. Luckily Lawley's big nostrils were glowing red like traffic lights, showing them the way. Rocks jutted out from the walls and stones littered the path. The air grew warmer, like a steamy bathroom.

Sam thought that he could hear someone singing. Yes, it was getting louder.

All of a sudden Lawley stopped. Sam bumped into his scaly tail and poor Dotty bumped into Sam. Sam was glad to feel her wagging tail tickling his legs.

'Sh! Granpa Doc is here in his pool.' Lawley whispered. 'He is used to being quiet so please don't shout or bark.'

Peeping round Lawley's tail, Sam could see a huge cave filled with a green fog. In the middle was a pool of steaming purple porridge. Bubbles came up to the surface then burst with a plopping sound.

Right in the middle of the magical pool was the biggest bubble that Sam had ever seen. It looked like a giant purple toad. The bubble was singing,

'Lipperty lop, plipperty, plop, hushily hushily hoo,
Slipperty slop, flipperty flop, cushily cushily coo.'

'Granpa Doc is so old that he lives in his pool all the time. If he didn't his skin would dry out and crack into a million pieces.' Lawley turned and spoke to the big bubble. It gurgled back in a stream of smaller bubbles. Then Sam noticed a head-like shape at one end with *two red nostrils* just like Lawley's. Sam was excited.

'Lawley, he looks like you. Please tell him it's great to meet him. Oh and thank him for his magic.'

To Sam's surprise the bubble began to to speak ...

'Saaammm, Dootteeeee.' Granpa knew their names, it must be the magic working. He crept nearer to the pool. A purple toad-like foot pushed something towards him. It waved once and slowly sank, the big bubble disappeared too. The pool was silent and still. Sam felt sad. The cave was cold and dark now Granpa Doc had gone.

'Goodbye Granpa Doc,' whispered Sam. Lawley scooped up the pebble that lay on the edge of the pool and told Sam to put it in his pocket.

'It's a special gift from Granpa Doc. Come, we must hurry before the magic fades.'

Lawley whisked them both on to his back, stretched out his wings and ... ...

Sam didn't remember what happened next because there was a rush of cold air and he found himself, Dotty and Lawley sitting in the orchard again.

'What does Granpa Doc look like? I only saw his nose like yours.'

'His body is as old as a fossil so he rests or moves slowly in his purple porridge pool. But he can send his magic anywhere. He *knows* when someone in his tribe is in danger. And I must be gone, Gramps is calling you.'

'Sam it's Friday remember, bath-night. And Dotty looks as if she needs a good rub down. What a grubby pair you make.'

# *DRAGON MAGIC AT STIPERSTONES*

Next morning Lawley heard Sam and Dotty running up the orchard.

'I want to show you the teeth of the White Dragons,' he said.

'Where are they? How far is it? I can walk miles and so can Dotty.'

Mm, thought the giant lizard dragon. Those little legs won't get us anywhere before tea time. I'll need to speed things up.

'Come on. Let's start right away.' He wound his great tail round them both and sat them down on his broad scaly back. Sam felt scared, dragons are fierce. In a flash they were flying. Below they saw Gramps poking his bonfire; they could even smell the smoke. Over the steep Long Mynd hills they went then tumbled down to land on a rocky hillside.

'Look, those are the White Dragons teeth,' Lawley was pointing at a line of jagged rocks.

Sam chuckled, 'They need a good clean. But where are the dragons?'

'Long ago the White Dragons of the Quartzeetees tribe were frozen solid in great ice sheets. Gradually they cracked into pieces and only this row of higgledy, piggledy teeth remain. They were such beautiful magical creatures.'

'Magic? Do you think any magic has been left behind?' Sam asked.

Lawley bent down close to Sam and whispered, 'I'll see what I can do.' Dotty and Sam crouched beside one of the rocks while the lizard dragon climbed on to the biggest one.

There was a chill in the air and a strong smell of smoke. Lawley mumbled some words. The wind caught them and blew them past the boy and his dog.

'Quartzeetees, Quartzeetees come show us your power,
Let us meet Wild Edric, just for this hour.'

All at once great white clouds gathered. Sam watched them change into icy cold dragons with feathery wings. They must be the Stiperstone White Dragons thought Sam but a moment later they were whisked away by the wind.

Everything went quiet. Dotty gave a sharp bark then Sam heard a noise. Who is tap, tapping? Where are they? The noises seemed to be under his feet.

Lawley came closer, 'We must move quickly while the magic lasts. Follow me.'

The lizard dragon walked straight through the rocky tooth and so did Sam and Dotty. As they went down the flight of steps the tap tapping noise grew louder.

'I can see someone,' whispered Sam. 'I'm sure he's making the tapping sound.'

An old man turned and stared at them. He was dressed in a sheepskin, his dark hair hung in tangled curls like a collar. He straightened his back then his face softened when he saw Lawley. Words poured from their lips but poor Sam could not understand what they were saying.

Lawley introduced Sam to the old man.

'This is Wild Edric. The White Dragons warned him that we were coming. He welcomes you to his home.' Lawley told them to follow Edric along the dark passages. A faint light glimmered in the distance. At last it opened out into a cave with a blazing fire. A lady sat brushing her hair which shone with stars in the firelight. Her dress was soft green like the new beech leaves in Springtime. She was humming gently. Sam yawned, it was a lullaby song, he felt sleepy. The lady looked up and smiled at Sam as Dotty curled up and fell asleep at her feet.

Lawley took Sam's hand and drew him towards the lady,

'This is Edric's wife, the Fairy Godda.' No wonder Sam had felt magic in the air. Here was a real fairy living underground. He stared and stared.

'Come on Sam, Edric wants you to meet his wild horses.'

The old man led them along more passages until they stood in a large cave. It was an underground yard with stables along one side. Wild, white horses were pawing the ground and shaking their silvery manes. They were ready to go.

'They're beautiful, said Sam, 'but where do you ride them?'

Without a word, Edric led the tallest horse from its stable and Lawley lifted Sam on to its back. The horse began to trot round the yard and Sam felt like a king.

Sam whispered to his friend, 'I wish I could talk with Edric.'

A deep voice boomed across the yard, 'Come we will ride together. Firelight will carry you safely, young Sam. Moonlight and I will take you along the Ridgeway.'

Sam *could* understand what Edric was saying. They rode through a door in the rocks. Moonlight led the way with Firelight following, their hooves clip clopping over the yard.

Once out on the Stiperstone hillside cold wind blew their hair and the horses' manes were streamers. Billowing wind pushed against them at every stride.

'Oh, Edric this is great. Thank you. I feel as if I'm flying on this magic horse.'

The horses raced faster across the ridge, forcing a path through the wild wind. Were they going a hundred miles an hour, thought Sam? Just then he heard Edric calling to the horses to slow down. Sam saw that they were back at the Stiperstone rocks.

'I'm sorry Sam, we must return to the stables. You see I usually exercise the horses under the darkness of the night. People of the villages around know that if Edric is *seen* riding on the ridge it is a warning of disaster.

Long ago I lost an important battle and my punishment means that I have to work in the lead mines by day and guard this place at night. Fairy Godda and I ride along here every night. We can raise an army in minutes.'

With his fist in the air Edric shouted, 'Never again will I lose the fight.'

'But Edric you have the best horses, you will always win. And I don't think you are *Wild Edric,* except when the wind tangles your hair.' Everybody laughed.

Back underground Sam found Dotty still fast asleep at Fairy Godda's feet.

'Edric has always been a good horseman. He found me one night long ago when I was dancing with my Fairy sisters. He knocked and came into the house but my sisters faded away. He looked a strong brave man and I fell in love with him.

We 've lived together for many, many years. Now, I help him keep these hills safe.'

Suddenly a huge ring of smoke rose up from the fairy's fire and curled round Dotty and Sam. Lawley said it was warning them that the hour was almost gone.

'Save your questions till next time Sam. Take this and keep it safe until we meet again.' whispered Fairy Godda.

How does she *know* my head is full of questions? thought Sam. It suppose its her fairy magic.

Lawley whisked his two friends along the passageways and out into the daylight. Edric and Fairy Godda waved them goodbye and off Lawley flew as fast as the wind. He landed just as Gramps was coming along the path with his wheelbarrow.

Sam was holding his gift in his hand and Gramps asked.

'What have you there, young Sam?' In his hand was a sparkly stone but he couldn't tell Gramps it was a fairy gift. Gramps would never believe him, would he.

'Mm we must look that up in my book after tea. Better go indoors now, Gran's waiting for us.'

# *SHREWSBURY SHOEMAKER*

Six weeks had passed before Sam visited Gran and Gramps again. Lawley had been lying in his pool dreaming up adventures. Sometimes he marched along the hill singing his songs. No one heard him. How he missed his friends.

As soon as Sam arrived, he ran up the garden shouting Lawley's name. The cheeky lizard dragon was sitting on a pile of stones with a big grin on his face. His eyes were full of mischief.

'Oh Sam, I thought you'd never come back. Come on, let's have fun.'

Sam sat on Lawley's tail. The lizard dragon lifted him up high and dropped him down so quickly, it made Sam squeal.

'Ow, my tummy's gone funny.' They all laughed. 'Do it again Lawley, please.'

After three goes, Lawley told Sam and Dotty that he would like to take them to Story Time.

'Granpa Doc's magic will carry us there, but you must remember this...

… Hold on tight
As you ride on my tail,
Close your eyes tight
Or the magic will fail.'

In Story Time we can all be *seen* and *heard*, so take care. Do you understand?'

Sam and Dotty nodded. Lawley lifted them on to his back, and then shouted, 'Off we go.' Wind whistled passed Sam's ears and Dotty's tail waved in the rush of air. Both held on tightly and kept their eyes shut.

At first Sam could hear lorries rumbling and motor bikes roaring past then everything suddenly changed. He could only hear birds singing and someone whistling as Lawley slowed down and stopped. It felt as if they were all sitting in a rocking chair.

When Lawley told them to open their eyes, Sam found out why. They were sitting in the topmost branches of a big oak tree. The branches were swaying in the breeze. Luckily they were well hidden by the leaves. The whistling was coming from below. Who was it? They were too frightened to move.

An old man dressed in rough clothes was whistling as he walked the path with a lumpy sack on his back.

He dropped it on the ground beneath the oak tree, then sat down and leant against the trunk.

'I'm getting too old to carry loads like this. I know missus says, Bodkin don't fill it so full. But she's glad of my wages, every little helps.' He untied the sack.

Sam could see it was full to the top. The man must be a shoemaker, thought Sam as he watched him check each one. There were shoes of all shapes and sizes. Some had buckles, some had laces and some were satin with buttons for ladies. But he couldn't see any trainers or football boots. Why?

The shoemaker pulled a red spotted bundle from his pocket. He untied the knot and inside Sam saw a chunk of cheese, a large slice of bread and an apple. It was Bodkin's lunch. Sam felt hungry too.

After his food, the shoemaker yawned and lay back against the trunk and closed his eyes for his midday nap. But Sam heard a louder noise which woke the shoemaker. Heavy footsteps were coming nearer; the shoemaker jumped to his feet.

'Goodness gracious me. Oh heavens above it can't be that giant, can it?' He was so afraid he was shaking. 'Can't hide. No time. Keep calm Bodkin, think. Come on, pull yourself together, what would the missus say?'

Sam felt sorry for the shoemaker. Even the leaves were quivering now, the stumbling footsteps came closer. Then Sam saw him. A huge giant was carrying a massive spade full of earth. He was grumbling to himself. The giant was in a bad mood.

'I hate the town of Shrewsbury. I'll dam their river with this soil and flood the place. That'll teach them a lesson.' He chuckled. 'I can't wait to see those people scurry around like a swarm of ants in the water. All their belongings will float away, serves them right. But I *must* be nearly there by now.

I've walked all the way from Wales and it can't be much further. I must sit down and rest.'

Suddenly he noticed the old man sitting by the tree with his fat sack. Ah, treasure he thought and in a polite voice asked,

'Pray where are you going with such a heavy load, my man?'

'I'm on my way home, great giant. Where might you be heading?'

'Shrewsbury, I'm visiting the town. Pray tell me how far does it lie? How long before I reach the river?'

Now the shoemaker had to act quickly if he was to outwit the giant. He began pulling all the shoes out of his sack and said in his weariest voice,

'Great giant, I have been to Shrewsbury and these are all the shoes I have worn out along the way. Yes, a whole sackful of shoes.'

That wicked giant slumped down on the track with a crash. His feet ached. If the old man had worn out a whole sackful of shoes, the town must be miles away.

'Oh dear, I can't walk that far I'm much too tired. I'll rest awhile then go back home.' He sat looking at the ground. He *was* disappointed. There was no treasure to steal in the sack, no river to flood and no damage to be done. Everything was going wrong.

With an enormous sigh, the giant fell asleep. Bodkin tied up his sack and set off along the track, whistling as he walked.

The giant woke after his nap and noticed his spade full of earth. He let out a long moan.

'Oh I'd forgotten that spadeful. It's no good I'll just have to drop it on the edge of the wood.'

Sam and Dotty watched him tip a hill-sized pile of earth, then he scraped off a smaller mound a bit further on. It was then that Sam noticed the shoemaker in the far distance How clever Bodkin had been to save Shrewsbury from a big flood.

Without thinking Sam stood up in the top of the oak tree and shouted as loud as he could 'Three cheers for Bodkin. Hip, hip hooray. Hip, hip hooray. Hip …'

The shoemaker turned to wave, he'd heard their shout but so had the giant who came stomping back in a great rage. He could see Sam and Dotty but Lawley was hidden in the leaves. He reached out his fat hand to grab them...

Whoosh! The next moment Sam and Dotty were on the lizard dragon's back and he was telling them to close their eyes tight and hold on. Just as the giant hand caught Sam's foot Lawley flew higher and they escaped.

'Eyes open, you two,' said Lawley, 'we're back home. Thank goodness Granpa Doc's magic worked.'

'Wow that was scary. The giant must be wondering where we have gone.'

'Bye now.' said Lawley and he flew off thinking he must be more careful next time.

# *HARVEST AT LEEBOTWOOD*

It was September. Sam had come to help Gran with the Harvest Festival. Together they piled apples into baskets, tied carrots into bunches, found three marrows and filled a box with shiny red tomatoes. The car was full. It didn't take long to reach the village church.

Inside, the church smell was different, not a damp musty smell but the scent of petals, wet leaves and fruit. Ladies were busy decorating every corner. Jars full of flowers were hanging above each other in pillars of colour near the altar. Apples and pears were hidden amongst cabbages, daisies and bunches of grapes hung from the gallery.

Gran was busy, so what could Sam do? He spied a green marrow with a curly end; it gave him an idea. He found two cabbage leaves and two black grapes on the floor. Someone had left some used matches on a window sill. Sam knew these would be useful.

He pushed a cabbage leaf into each side of the marrow for wings. Each grape he spiked with a matchstick and pushed them into one end as eyes. A broken carrot made a good snout and a thin parsnip became a long tail at the curly end. As he stood looking at his creature someone whispered,

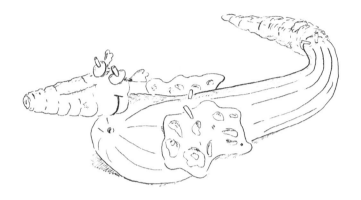

'What a fierce dragon you've made and look at his cheeky black eyes.'

Gran was pleased that Sam was busy too.

Mrs. Andover called out, 'Rose, I could do with your help.'

'Put your bits in the bin, I won't be long,' said Gran.

But Sam wasn't listening. He was turning Granpa Doc's pebble over and over in his pocket. He was thinking of Lawley and wondering if *he* would like the marrow dragon.

Suddenly a gust of wind caught the church door and rattled it against the iron doorstop. Notice sheets came to life and flew up like white birds. A handful of dry leaves blew up the aisle, fluttered round and landed on top of the marrow dragon. A waft of warm air blew against Sam's ear. He turned and saw Lawley standing beside him, grinning from ear to ear.

'Wow, I look great. I like the curly tail.'

'But how did you know where I was? 'asked Sam.

'I heard your wish as you turned Granpa's pebble. I came at once.'

Sam was glad that Lawley was invisible. The ladies would have screamed in fright to see a dragon in church.

A boy pushed past Sam and walked right through Lawley's tail..

'Hey, that's clever, your marrow dragon. Let's hide it between the flowers on the front table. I bet no one has ever seen a dragon at the harvest before. They'll think one of those ladies did it.' The boy chuckled mischievously.

Before Sam had time to agree, the boy had pushed the marrow dragon right in the centre of the harvest display.

'Come on quick before they see us,' he whispered, grabbing Sam's shirt and pulled him down behind a pew. They waited to see what would happen.

'I'm Jim Cooper, what's your name?'

'Sam Williams. Gran's over there, I'm staying with her this weekend to help with the harvest.'

Jim told Sam that he had come to carry stuff for his gran too. He pulled a face and said in a squeaky voice, 'Just you be a good boy now.'

Sam laughed, 'Grandmothers always say things like that.'

All this time he had been watching Lawley but he couldn't speak to him, not with Jim so close by.

'We could go up into the gallery, they won't see us up there,' said Jim. Sam followed him through a door. Giggling all the way the two boys crawled up the narrow staircase like toddlers.

'Gosh it's like a secret hiding place,' said Sam. 'I didn't see this when I came in.'

It was dark in the gallery. They were close to the roof, under the beams. A good place for spiders and bats, thought Sam. Jim switched a light on.

'Look up there, on the beam,' said Jim. 'can you see the two dragons? My gran looks out for them when she does the cleaning. *Morning dragons, you still there?* she says.'Sam stared and stared. Gradually he could make out two dragons carved on the beam, their snouts pointing to the middle of the roof. They had curly tails and wings just like his marrow dragon.

'Gran told me they used to be red, green and gold but the colour has all worn off. They are very old.'

Making sure that Jim wouldn't see him, Sam leant over the balcony and waved to Lawley. A swirl of leaves blew up into the roof and landed at his feet. The lizard dragon had arrived!

'Jim, where are you? Come and help me carry these boxes.'

'Gran needs me, back in two ticks.' Jim dashed down the stairs.

Sam turned to Lawley. 'Phew just in time, now we can talk. Best be quick before he comes back.'

'I wondered if you'd notice my friends in the roof,'said the lizard dragon. He had a big grin on his face.' They also belong to the Magma tribe but they cannot come back to life. This one is Lee and the other one is Bot. Granpa Doc made them the guardians of the village and they keep watch from the church.'

'I'm glad *you* are alive,' said Sam,

'And me, but I must be off.' In a whoosh of leaves Lawley was gone, leaving Sam in a cloud of dust.

'Golly that was a hurricane,' gasped Jim. 'gran told me off for leaving the doors open when the wind rushed past me.' Sam just smiled.

'I've had an idea,' said Sam. 'let's call these dragons Lee and Bot. I've made up a song for them.' ..

'Here is Lee and there is Bot,
Who are they? Two dragons? What?

Two brave dragons, carved in wood
Guard this church as they should.

Once shone red, green and gold
All rubbed off, they're so old.

Lee to the left, Bot to the right
Climb to the gallery,
But switch on the light!'

Jim joined in and their singing became louder and louder, especially *'switch on the light.* It changed to a marching song until a grown-up suggested it would be better if the soldiers marched along the church path outside. They had great fun. All too soon it was lunchtime and they both had to go home.

'See you tomorrow at the Harvest Festival,' shouted Jim as he ran to the car.

Jim's gran was telling him to 'hurry up and don't shout so loud.' Poor Jim was always in trouble.

Next day was the Harvest Service in the Leebotwood church. By the time Gran, Gramps and Sam arrived, people were already in their seats. They squeezed in at the end of a row. Sam could see Jim through a gap and they waved to each other. He was squashed between his gran and Mrs. Andover, whose feathery hat kept tickling his hair.

Sam couldn't see much so he fiddled with a piece of straw he'd found. Then he felt Granpa Doc's pebble in his pocket and turned it over and over. It was so smooth. It reminded him of Lawley when suddenly he heard the vicar's loud voice,

'Dragons. Well it's the first time we have had a dragon on our Harvest display. This is a marvellous marrow-dragon. I understand it was made by Sam the grandson of Mr. and Mrs. Williams. Well done young man. Aaah choo'. Then the vicar sneezed again twice more.

A whirlwind of dry leaves and dust was spinning through the church. Oh no, thought Sam, it must be Lawley again. Sure enough Sam looked round and he couldn't help smiling. Lawley was sitting up in the gallery with his legs dangling over the edge eating a bunch of grapes. On his head he wore Mrs. Andover's feathery hat. *She* was searching under her seat trying to find out where it had gone.

Sam signalled to Jim and pointed to the roof. Jim saw the feathery hat caught up near the dragon beam. He collapsed into giggles. But his gran nudged him and said,'Behave yourself or you'll be sent out my lad.' Jim managed to sit still but found it hard to stop laughing.

After the service everyone was talking about the 'flying hat' and wondering where that wind had come from. Sam looked at Gran, she was smiling to herself as she stared at the gallery. Could Gran have *seen* Lawley wearing that awful hat full of feathers?

# SH! IPPIKIN WILL CATCH YOU

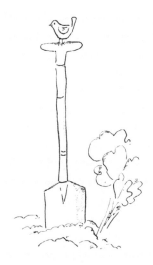

Sam had been busy all morning. Gramps needed help with digging up the potatoes.

It was a muddy job, mud everywhere. Even Gramps had slipped over so they both had to change their trousers at lunch time.

After he'd eaten, Sam took Dotty up the garden to find Lawley. The lizard dragon was sitting on top of the rock pile. He did laugh when he heard about them slipping and sliding in the mud.

'Whatever were you doing?'

'We were digging up *treasure,*' said Sam. 'Gramps calls his potatoes his treasure because he plants one in each hole and when he digs it up later... hey presto there are loads. Look this is the biggest one of all.'

'Not as big as me, said Lawley. 'I can show you someone in Story Time who loves treasure. Would you like to go on..?' Before Lawley had finished his question, Sam and Dotty were climbing on to his back.

'All aboard and remember...
Hold on tight
As you ride on my tail.
Close your eyes
Or the magic will fail.'

There was a rushing sound followed by a bump. Sam and Dotty opened their eyes and looked around. They were sitting in a tree, high up on a ridge. Someone was coming along the track. No need to worry, they were well hidden.

A young man came into sight. He was carrying a bundle on his back. His boots were muddy and worn as if he'd travelled a long way.

'Oh I'm tired. Not far now, just past Ippikin's Rock then down the valley and home.'

Without warning a scruffy little man jumped out of the bushes and knocked the traveller to the ground. The robber ran off with the bundle, leaving the young man bruised and bleeding.

'Oh no! All my money has gone and my precious gold chain. Whatever will Father say when I get home?' He struggled to his feet, 'I should have known better than to mention that name.' He wiped his face with his hanky and brushed dust from his clothes. As he limped along the road that young man didn't know that a boy and a dog were watching and how much they wished they could help him.

Sam climbed down and crossed the track. He peered over the edge.

Halfway down on a ledge, sat the robber. He was trying to undo the bundle. Soon he pulled out a silver tankard and a fat leather purse. He chuckled as he tipped out several silver coins and a shiny gold chain. The scruffy little man began to dance and shout for joy at his good fortune. Sam noticed his spiky red hair and *his chin*. It was the longest chin he'd ever seen. Sam shivered. He did not want to get caught by this nasty little man.

All of a sudden there was a loud rumble, stones and earth came crashing down. Sam grabbed a branch and held on tight. But the scruffy little man and his treasure had disappeared. As the dust cleared, Sam could see a large boulder half way down the slope. He could hear noises. Sam looked across to Lawley.

'Can you hear them arguing? Who are they?'

'Well, that is Ippikin's rock. There's a cave behind that boulder. I'll fly you closer if you jump on my tail. We'll find out what's going on.'

Sam was frightened but Lawley dug his toes deep into the earth to hold them steady while the three friends listened.

'Why are we still in this cave Ippikin? We've been here for years.'

'Your missus will have a shock when you do get out Pinchbags. Your beard is down to the floor.'

'Shut up you two, let Ippikin speak.'

'Now listen here, you miserable lot. We have gold today, thanks to me. If we're lucky someone else might call out my name and I can grab more treasure.'

The arguments began again with everyone squabbling over how much gold each one should have.

'We must be ready. When someone calls my name you lot push this rock as hard as you can. We *must* break the spell and escape. Come on now, three cheers for Ippikin and his band of robbers'

Loud cheers deafened Dotty but Lawley was telling Sam the story of Ippikin.

'Ippikin was once a knight but he grew so greedy that he started robbing travellers. If anyone calls his name he robs them but a spell throws him back into the cave.'

That naughty lizard dragon was grinning. He wanted to make mischief.

'Why don't *we* try calling his name?'

Sam shook his head, that was not a good idea. But Lawley took no notice. Sam felt in his pocket and found Granpa Doc's pebble. He might need it.

'Of course we'll be fine. Remember I am Lawley the Giant Lizard Dragon.'

Oh dear thought Sam, when Lawley starts boasting things always go wrong.

'Sit on my tail and we'll practice shouting.' They sang the Lee and Bot marching song loudly and the Pimple song even louder. Then that naughty lizard dragon shouted out,

'**Ippikin, Ippikin** red-haired **Ippikin**,
Keep away with your chinny, chin chinnigen.'

A great cloud of dust blew up and as it cleared Sam saw that wicked robber running towards them. 'Watch out Lawley, he's got a stick with a hook.'

The hook caught in Sam's shoe. He felt himself being pulled down closer and closer to the cave. He held his pebble tight and wished. Lawley gave a great roar and breathing fierce flames he managed to push the boulder back across the cave entrance. Ippikin and his robbers were prisoners once more.

Sam and Dotty had their eyes closed as they hurtled through a magic storm. It felt as if they were being sucked down a giant plughole. Lawley landed with a bump near Gramps' shed.

'Phew that was scary. I didn't want to be a prisoner in the robbers' cave. Thank goodness Granpa Doc's magic saved us in time,' said Sam.

Lawley nodded and chuckled, 'But it *was* fun, wasn't it.'

# GRAN'S SECRET

The alarm woke Sam next morning. He had overslept. He grabbed his clothes and shot into the bathroom. After a quick rub round his face with the flannel, Sam pulled on his trousers and T- shirt. Something clanked near the wash basin but there was no time to look. He wanted to see Lawley.

'Morning Gran, sorry I'm late but I ...' before he could finish his sentence Gran had put a bowl of crispies in front of him. He gobbled them up quickly and shouted, 'I'm off now, come on Dotty.'

Gran smiled to herself. School holidays were fun. She remembered those exciting days but she mustn't stand around dreaming. There's work to be done.

The bathroom needed cleaning first. How could one boy make such a mess with just soap and water? She wiped bubbles off the mirror, puddles off the floor and slippery soap slides near the wash basin. Clank! Surely soap wouldn't make that sort of noise. She felt round the pedestal and felt something hard. It was a pebble.

Now Sam was the last one in the bathroom, he must have dropped it.

Gran turned the pebble over. She gasped. She had seen something like this before, many years ago. It was a fossil stone from the quarry. Oh dear, Gran began to worry. Had Sam been playing near there? Where was he now? She put the pebble on the landing cupboard for safe keeping.

Meanwhile Sam was sitting at the top of the garden talking to Lawley. They were laughing about Ippikin and his friends. When Sam put his hand in his pocket to find his magic pebble, it wasn't there. He pulled out bits of grass, a snail shell, a rubber band and a stubby bit of red crayon. But there wasn't a pebble.

'Wait a minute,' he shouted, 'I remember something fell on the bathroom floor. Sorry you two I must go and look.' And in a flash he was off down the orchard.

Crash went the kitchen door, Gran jumped and nearly knocked the teapot over.

'Why such a rush, Sam? Are you being chased by a bull?'

'Sorry Gran, I need to go to the bathroom quickly,' Sam shouted. Seeing her worried face, he popped his head round the door and laughed.

'I'm okay. I haven't got stomach ache. I lost something important this morning. I think it's in the bathroom.'

Before Gran had time to blink Sam was leaping up the stairs two at a time. He sounded like a herd of elephants. Cupboard doors were opened and closed with a crash. Even the toilet lid was flipped up and down. She could hear scrabbling noises under the bath like giant mice.

Then slow heavy footsteps coming down the stairs told Gran what she already knew. Sam had found nothing.

'Why didn't you ask me before you dashed off?' she said. 'Just turn round and this time tip toe up the stairs. Look on the landing cupboard. I think you'll find what you're looking for.'

There was a shout of joy. Sam rushed into the kitchen. He flung his arms round Gran and hugged her tight.

'Hey, you're squashing me. Let me see what you were worrying about.'

'It's a special pebble, a friend gave it to me.' Sam was struggling. It was a secret. What could he tell her?

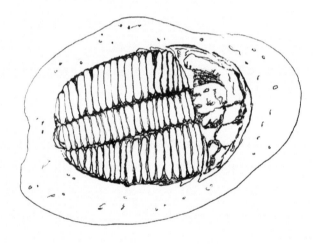

'Have you been playing near the old quarry Sam? Tell me the truth.'

'No, I never go near there, it's too dangerous. I'm not stupid, Gran.'

'That's good to know. So tell me more.'

Sam opened his hand and showed her Granpa Doc's special stone.

Gran turned it over and began humming to herself. 'Mm Mm that's very interesting, Mm.'

'Look it has a shape scratched on the back,' said Sam.

'That's a fossil,' said Gran. 'It was a creature like our wood louse which got trapped in this rock. It is called a Trilobite. But who gave it to you, Sam?'

He didn't hear her question. He was bursting with excitement as he said, 'Do you know what Gran, It's a magic pebble *and* it's a secret.'

Before Sam could say another word, Gran took something out of her apron pocket and put it on the kitchen table. It was a pebble like his, only much smaller. He lay his pebble beside Gran's and turned them both over to show the fossil side. He looked at Gran. Her eyes were twinkling and then she burst out laughing and gave Sam a big hug.

'When I was a young girl, the man next door worked in the old quarry. One day he found this pebble and gave it to me. Would you believe it, it's the same Trilobite fossil as yours.'

Sam wanted to ask Gran lots of questions. Was her stone magic? Had she seen any of Granpa Doc's tribe? But just at that moment the kitchen door opened and in came Gramps for his mid-morning drink.

'Where's my hot chocolate Rose? Have you forgotten the time?'

He shook his head,'Ah she's been showing you her keepsakes, has she? Filling your head with stories I've no doubt. She's had that pebble in her apron pocket as long as I've known her. Now where's my drink, young man?'

'Fetch three mugs please Sam and as soon as you have had your drink off you go and play. I must finish my cleaning or Gramps will be complaining.' Gran winked at Sam and they all laughed.

# WHERE ARE THE MATCHES?

November the fifth began with a bright and frosty morning. Sam was up early; he wanted to help Gramps make a bonfire. They fetched paper and cardboard boxes from the shed. Sam piled logs and branches in the wheelbarrow and Gramps began building the fire. It looked like a wigwam. Gramps loved bonfires. Sometimes they would burn all day long. Gran would shoo him out of her kitchen, complaining that he smelled like a bonfire.

Sam helped Gramps to fill buckets of water and carry them into the field.

'Just in case the flames spread too far,' said Gramps. Water slopped over Sam's boots. It was hard carrying buckets of water when it kept sloshing this way and that! He was glad to run off and play afterwards.

Lawley saw Sam and Dotty running up the orchard. When he heard Sam's news about the bonfire he was very excited. But what did he mean about eating 'hot dogs'?

'Don't be silly Lawley,' said Sam. 'Hot dogs' are cooked sausages in bread with lots of tomato sauce. You didn't really think we would cook Dotty, did you?'

Lawley shook his head and asked 'But what time will we light the bonfire? Shall I come at three o' clock or four or five?' He was jumping up and down; he was so excited.

'No, make sure it's really dark. Come at six o' clock.' Poor Sam did not want the lizard dragon to upset everything. Remember, when Lawley gets too excited that's when things go wrong.

Sam and Dotty raced through the orchard but as they passed Gramps' shed he shouted, 'Hey, you're just in time to help me with the lantern.'

On the bench sat a big yellow pumpkin. Gramps had cut a slice off the top and was scooping out the inside, 'Pass me that basin please Sam. This will make lovely soup.'

Next he carved two eyes and a triangular nose. He gave the face a big grin and popped a night light inside. 'There we're all done. We must find a safe place that's quiet for Dotty and then it's toast for tea. Not long now before we light the fire.'

The sky grew darker about six o' clock and the air was chilly. Sam and Gran stood back as Gramps struck the first match. Soon flames licked the cardboard boxes and twigs crackled.

One side of the fire seemed to burn more quickly, then it suddenly roared. Whoosh!

A cloud of steam flew up, Gramps had thrown a bucket of water over it.

'Don't worry, I've doused the flames,' shouted Gramps. 'They were going too close to the hedge. I don't know where the wind came from.'

Sam looked round and *he knew*. He had forgotten Lawley in his excitement and saw that naughty lizard dragon puffing out his cheeks ready to blow again. Sam shook his head and stopped him.

'Let's have some sparklers. Give the lad one,' said Gramps. Gran opened the box of matches to light the firework, but the box was empty.

'Where's the spare box of matches?' she asked. Poor Gramps made his way back to the shed, grumbling all the way. As soon as Gramps was out of sight, Sam's sparkler burst into life... *all by itself.*

There was a loud chuckle. Lawley was up to his old tricks. He had used his hot breath to set the sparkler alight.

'Sh!Sh! You are not supposed to be seen or heard,' whispered Sam. Gran pricked up her ears. She could hear voices but whose were they? Through the hazy smoke, she could see a dragon shape. This creature was causing all the noise and Sam *was talking to it.*

In a flash she remembered seeing this same dragon wearing Mrs. Andover's hat at the Harvest Festival. She couldn't help smiling even though he was very naughty indeed.

A loud bang made them all jump. A green ball shot up from the fire. It flew high in the sky and burst in a shower of sparkling snowflakes. A whirring sound followed as a huge Catherine Wheel rolled out from the flames. On and on it went round the field in a cloud of coloured stars until it exploded with an even louder BANG! Lawley loved fireworks and he was getting more and more excited.

He sent an enormous rocket hurtling into the sky, showering everything in golden dust. It passed over the village in a stream of silver stars. On and on it went over the hills, until it disappeared in a magic rainbow above Granpa Doc's hill.

Sam and Gran heard the dragon singing,

'Blue and green, yellow and red,
All the best colours
Over Granpa Doc's head.

He's so clever, big and tall'
No one better, they're all small.

Three cheers for LAWLEY,
The greatest dragon there is.

Bang, Bang, Bang, Bang
Whizz, Whizz, Whizzzzzzz

As the sounds fizzled out, everything fell silent. Sam looked round and so did Gran. There was no sign of Lawley. Suddenly someone coughed.

'Ah, that made you jump,' said Gramps. 'sorry it took me so long, I found them outside the shed by the pumpkin lantern.

Oh no! Lawley had seen the lantern. Sam could see him skipping along the hedge with it balancing on his head. Luckily Gramps hadn't noticed.

'Did you see those spectacular fireworks Sam? Someone must have spent a fortune.'

Gran squeezed Sam's hand. He was sure she could see Lawley now.

'Well you two, do you want these sparklers or not?'

'I'll have one,' said Gran. 'Let's see whose lasts the longest.'

Gramps lit all three but they sent out clouds of smoke. He tried another match but still nothing happened. Poor Gramps was so disappointed that he threw them into the bonfire.

Immediately they came to life, twirling on their wire stalks. They had ribbons of yellow and red, then blue and purple balls danced in the sky. The wind carried the swirling colours into a dragon shaped cloud high up in the sky. Sam smiled, he knew where Lawley had gone. That cheeky lizard dragon was showing off again.

Gramps stood with his mouth wide open but no words came. His eyes were popping with astonishment. The fireworks were not dud ones. No, they were the best ones ever.

'Wow Gramps, those sparklers were magic.'

Gramps beamed with pleasure. He was overjoyed. Gran handed him the biggest hot dog as a 'thank you.' Sam enjoyed squeezing plenty of tomato sauce into his and on the jacket potato.

Gradually the flames died down. A few sparks spat from the embers as Sam crept over to give Lawley the last hot dog. He smiled and with his mouth full of sausage he nodded his thanks. Sam burst out laughing as tomato sauce dribbled down his snout and dripped on the tip of his tail.

With only a faint glow from the ashes, they all knew it was time to go indoors. Sam looked back to see Lawley blowing smoke rings and figures of eight from his nostrils. Trails of tiny sparks wafted through the rings. It had been a perfect night for a dragon with fire, flames and explosions.

Sam called to him, 'Good night Lawley, mind you don't burn your tail.' the lizard dragon waved to Sam, and cheekily blew a stream of stars right over his head and sent a circle of stardust round Gran.

Gramps didn't notice anything; he was still puzzling about those sparklers. he knew the packet label said 'Giant Dragon Sparklers' but he couldn't remember where he had bought them.

# MITCHELL THE WITCH

The three friends Dotty, Lawley and Sam were enjoying marching up and down the orchard singing songs at the top of their voices.

'Gosh I'm thirsty,' said Sam, 'I'd love a glass of milk.'

'I know where to find plenty of milk. We'll fly to Story Time. Jump on my tail. Eyes shut tight and remember *we* can be seen but the magic will keep us safe.'

In the space of three sneezes the lizard dragon and his passengers landed on a steep hillside. They could see fields and forests stretching far into the distance. But instead of juicy green grass everything was brown and dry. A bird was singing in a gorse bush and sheep were bleating. Where will we find milk up here, Sam wondered.

His question started the magic. The sun slipped lower in the sky turning the countryside pink. Scraggy sheep wandered off down the hill to find shelter for the night. An owl hooted. It was getting dark. Sam clutched his fossil stone, it was hidden deep in his pocket. It made him feel safe.

He heard voices and saw a line of people coming up the path. He quickly pulled Dotty out of sight behind the gorse. Mothers were chatting as their children chased one another. Everyone was carrying a bucket. Where were they going?

Close by an old man called out to a neighbour, 'Let's hope Bounty fills our buckets tonight Jo. I need a drink. Our well is dry. I bet yours is too.'

'Has been for a long while. But Bounty won't let us down as long as no one takes more than his share. One bucket each and no more that's her bargain.'

Sam noticed a small white cow standing patiently at the top of the hill. He was puzzled.

'How can one cow fill all these buckets with milk, Lawley?'

'I'll tell you what's happened. There has been no rain for weeks and the villagers' cows have died. The people have had very little to drink or eat. A wise woman from the village begged a good fairy to help them. She agreed to send a white cow called Bounty who would give every villager a bucket of milk at sunset. But, there was a warning,. .. *if anyone dares to take more than his or her share, the spell will break and Bounty the cow will be gone for ever.'*

Sam looked at the long line of people waiting their turn. Right at the end stood an old woman. She had stopped to catch her breath. She looked across to the bush where Sam was hiding. Could she see him? He shivered. Goose pimples prickled his arms. He did not like her.

When she picked up her bucket and moved on, Sam was glad.

'Phew, that was a lucky escape, thank goodness she's gone,' he said.

Bounty the white cow was standing patiently as each person took their share of milk. Soon it was the old woman's turn. She bent down and sat on the milking stool and straight away her wiry fingers began to squirt the milk into her bucket.

After a few minutes Sam wondered why her bucket wasn't full. Was it a magic bucket? Still the old woman went on milking the little cow. Suddenly he noticed a stream of milk trickling down the path. Forgetting he was in Story Time, Sam shouted, 'Stop, you're spilling it.' The old woman looked up and laughed.

'I'm Mitchell the witch,
I weave spells of my own
Bad ones not good ones
No smiles, only groans.
Come let down more milk dear.
I'll drain this cow dry,
She'll disappear for ever
Just watch them all cry.
Hocus, pocus, milk and cream,
Frothy bubbles blue and green.
Spell be broken, cow be gone
Mitchell the witch's spell is done.

There was a loud 'Screeeeeeech.' Sam covered his ears. It was the wicked witch. The little cow let out a long sad bellow. As the last spot of milk dropped on the ground, the bucket tipped over. It had holes in the bottom like a sieve. The fairy's spell was broken.

A whirlwind scooped up the white cow and whisked her away over the moon. In a mighty flash, the witch disappeared. Where she had been standing there was a large rock caught in a circle of smaller stones. A ring of thick green smoke drifted round them.

Lawley sat close by humming to himself as the last wisps of green smoke wafted from his nostrils.

'Could Mitchell the witch see me behind that bush?' asked Sam.

'Yes, but Granpa Doc's strongest magic saved us all. Don't worry Sam, she will never escape from that stone circle; that is her punishment.'

'What will happen to the villagers though?'

Lawley smiled, 'Look through the green smoke. What do you see?'

Sam stared as hard as he could. The green smoke was like a thick fog.

'I can't *see* much but I can *feel* something. It's starting to rain. I'm getting soaked. The grass is getting greener. The children are laughing and the farmer is putting two brown cows into the field. Some boys have brought buckets ready to start milking.'

The smoke was clearing and Sam looked at Lawley. They both smiled.

'The drought is over and life should be much happier for the village. Come along our time here is running out. Jump on my tail, eyes tightly shut and we must be gone.'

They landed by Gramps' shed. Sam looked around. That's funny he thought, it was night time in Story Time but it is still afternoon here. Then he forgot all about time and all about Lawley.

Sam was so thirsty that he raced down to the kitchen and found a tall glass. Dotty went straight to her water bowl. Sam filled his glass with... ... can you guess what he had to drink?

# MISCHIEF IN SHREWSBURY

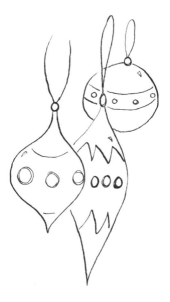

The water butts were frozen and ducks were sliding across their icy pool. Deep inside his hill Lawley wallowed in the hot steamy water of *his* pool. He realised when he heard shouts high above him that Sam had arrived. School holidays had begun.

They were so pleased to be together again. Dotty was jumping and yapping and Sam couldn't stop talking, While Lawley stood there with a wide grin on his face.

'What shall we do today?' asked Sam.

'We could fly to Shrewsbury and look in the toy shops.' There was a mischievous twinkle in Lawley's eye. No one noticed.

He lifted Sam and Dotty on to his back and they flew off way above the main road. It was busy with traffic. Here and there they saw windows with Christmas trees covered in sparkling lights. When they reached the town, street after street wore long necklaces of flickering lights, red and green, purple, orange and yellow.

They landed in the square amidst the bustling crowds. Children were singing carols and a band played 'Jingle Bells.'

Lawley started dancing in and out of the lamp posts and hitting huge flashing snowflakes with his tail. Thank goodness the magic made Lawley invisible to everyone, except Sam and Dotty of course.

Shops and offices shone with gold and silver baubles. It looked magical. People crowded the pavements struggling to get along as their bags were loaded with so many parcels.

'Come on you two slowcoaches,' Lawley shouted, as he pushed his way into a toy shop. He'd hardly got through the door when he saw a basket full of Santa hats. He grabbed one and stuck it on his head. Next he pushed a pair of red antlers on top and a big red nose on his snout.

A shopper asked how much they were. That naughty lizard dragon kept bobbing his head out of reach, as the shop girl tried to catch them.

'I'm sorry madam. Ask at the next counter they have some in a box.'

Sam giggled. Lawley *was* having fun. But, oh dear, Sam saw a pile of chocolate Father Christmases sliding on to the floor. He knew it was Lawley. There he sat nibbling one after another. Some little children joined him and a few minutes later only a pile of silver paper was left.

Lawley was off again, racing over to look at the big toys, battery cars and bicycles. People watched in amazement as the toys sped over the shop floor … on their own. Only Dotty and Sam knew who was riding them and pressing the buttons. Dolls began to cry and shout 'Mama' and tip upside down. Robots fired space guns sending out blue crackling flashes. Electric trains raced so fast they jumped off their tracks and collided with the speeding racing cars.

A loud speaker boomed out, 'Will everybody please leave the Toy Department immediately. This is an emergency. I repeat, this is an emergency.'

Sam grabbed Dotty's collar and helped her down the stairs and out into the street. Where was Lawley? Crowds on the pavement were staring up at the shop windows, as hats and curtains waved like flags. Trees full of fairy-lights chased teddy bears and a yellow car was spinning on its back wheels with sparks flying from its headlights. People started laughing as a giant panda jumped on top of the Christmas tree pushing the fairy on to the floor.

'Oh no,' Sam said aloud.'What will he do next? How can I stop him?' He rubbed the magic trilobite stone in his pocket.

Clouds of green smoke filled the windows and as it cleared only a mountain of toys was left. Some were upside down, others had twisted heads where their legs should be and the yellow car had no wheels except the steering wheel which was stuck on its boot. There was no sign of Lawley.

A blast of hot air tickled Sam's neck. He turned and saw Lawley standing beside him, smiling. Sam was about to tell him off when naughty Lawley shouted.

'That was good fun. I tried it all and now I'm going to see Father Christmas.'

In a flash, he was gone. Sam saw him on the escalator which was carrying people up to the top floor.

The stairs moved slowly upwards... then stopped halfway. People tried to get off, some walked up while others pushed past on their way down.

All of a sudden the escalator jerked and set off at great speed so no one could jump on. But Sam could see Lawley waving as he flew first to the top then bumped down to the bottom. Soon crowds gathered; everyone wanted to see the magic staircase.

Policemen arrived. They scratched their heads wondering what to do. They all laughed, because they didn't know how to stop it moving. So they put up a notice saying 'OUT OF ORDER'. As the people disappeared, Lawley didn't want to play any more so he jumped off the escalator which crashed down buckling the bottom steps.

'That was silly. You could have hurt yourself.'

But Lawley hadn't heard a word. He was running up the stairs with the 'OUT OF ORDER' sign hanging on his tail.

'I'm off to see Father Christmas,' he said as he jumped the stairs two at a time.

Mm, thought Sam, we'll see what Father Christmas thinks about that. I only have presents if I've been good.'

Sam and Dotty caught up with Lawley in the queue. Excited children were jumping up and down beside their mothers who were struggling with pushchairs and bulging shopping bags. And Lawley was standing quietly watching the children.

Suddenly that Giant Lizard dragon blew a smoke ring as big as a cloud which set off all the sprinklers. People were running everywhere, some people even put up umbrellas. What a noise, squealing and shrieking, and children crying. In a flash Lawley pressed the alarms and the water trickled to a stop.

What a shock for the poor firemen in their helmets pulling long water hoses.

They'd been told to come quickly the Toy Shop was on fire. Children clapped and shouted, 'There isn't a fire. The sprinklers came on all by themselves and we got soaked.'

A loud speaker boomed out, 'We are sorry about the incident.

Please will all parents and children come down to the lower floor where hot drinks and toast will be free for everyone. Father Christmas will start again after he has dried his coat and his beard.'

Lawley was first in the new queue. Sam watched as he squeezed through the door into Santa's grotto. What would happen to him? A few minutes later the lizard dragon appeared. He was not smiling.

Sam and Dotty took their turn straight away. They asked Father Christmas for their special gifts. Sam whispered, 'a bicycle,' and Dotty yapped, 'sausages.' The kind old man said that he'd try to make their wishes come true.

'Come on you two, we must be back for tea. I'll meet you outside the shop.'

Of course, Lawley was first so he lifted them on to his back and whoosh they were in the sky, looking down on the lights once more.

'What happened when *you* saw Father Christmas, Lawley? Could he *see* you? Was he angry?' Sam asked.

'Mm, I told him what I wanted, but he made me promise to be good every day *before* Christmas then I *might* have a present, but I'm not sure what it will be.'

'What did you wish for?'

'Ah, that's *my* secret, said Lawley,' hold tight we're nearly there.'

Sam heard Lawley whispering to the wind. *I'd like a race track with a racing car that goes a hundred miles an hour, a bicycle that turns into an aeroplane and an ice cream machine that never stops working... and a ...*

The wind was so strong that the words were whisked away. So you must imagine what else that Giant Lizard Dragon asked for. Did his wishes come true,

I wonder?

# STOKESAY GIANTS' TREASURE

Lawley was waiting for Sam and Dotty. Why were they so late?

He whacked the ground with his tail. They came running up through the orchard. Their paws and boots were wet with dew. They hardly had time to catch their breath before Lawley's tail caught them and whisked them on to the lizard dragon's back.

'All aboard, no time to waste. We're going to Story Time, so eyes closed and hold on tight.'

In no time at all they were falling down, down, down and landed with a bump. Sam looked round and saw the tower of a castle and a church and cottages nearby. A high wall ran round the castle. Sam and Dotty jumped down and ran alongside the wall to see what lay beyond it.

A loud noise echoing from the hills stopped them in their tracks. High above the castle stood a huge giant with arms outstretched. He was yawning.

'That's Hwittuc,' whispered Lawley.

'And there across the valley is his brother Frod.'

Sam started to giggle because tall Hwittuc had spiky hair like a hedgehog while short fat Frod was like a bouncy ball that kept chuckling to itself.

Hwittuc shouted, 'Brother Frod, please throw the key over to me.

I need money from the treasure chest to pay the shoemaker for my new boots.

Mind how you throw, remember we only have one key. We mustn't lose it.'

Frod stopped jumping and pulled a large key from his pocket. He swung himself round three times and threw the key high. It flew across the valley to land safely at Hwittuc's feet.

'Well done, that's your best throw ever.' Hwittuc pushed the key deep into his pocket and taking three huge strides he reached the wall of the castle. He stepped over it and crossed the courtyard to reach the North Tower.

The three friends crept closer. All was quiet, so quiet that they could hear the key squeak as it unlocked the cellar door. A loud 'caw' came from a black raven who seemed to be guarding the chest inside.

Hwittuc took a handful of corn from his pocket and threw it to the bird. Now he could unlock the chest in peace.

At that moment a shaft of sunlight lit the cellar. Sam couldn't believe his eyes. The treasure chest was full of gold coins, gold chains and golden fruit. A jackdaw also spied the shining coins. He knew this was real treasure.

'Mm, that should be enough to pay for my boots,' murmured Hwittuc as he poured a handful into his purse. He shut the lid and locked it. They all heard the key squeak as the giant closed the cellar door.

Hwittuc shouted up to Frod and invited him to come down.

'I can see the shoemaker coming. He has my smart new boots in his cart.'

Suddenly two things happened at once. Frod tripped on a stone and rolled head over heels down the hill and into the castle courtyard. At the same moment the shoemaker and his cart arrived too. The startled driver pulled hard on the reins and shouted 'Whoa,' thankfully he missed Frod.

The shoemaker and his boy dragged the big boots across the yard. Each one looked like a canoe. Hwittuc sat down and pulled off his old ones, then eased his feet into the new shiny ones. They were bright red and fitted perfectly.

As Hwittuc was paying his bill, Frod kept bouncing round the cart. He seemed very excited.

'Kind shoemaker, please measure my feet.
I'd like boots oh so, ever so neat.
A pair to carry me round and round
So my feet would hardly touch the ground.'

The shoemaker nodded. He measured the giant's feet and the boy wrote the sizes in the order book. All was agreed and they set off back to Shrewsbury.

Dear reader remember this is Story Time and here time passes in the blink of an eye.

Sam saw the shoemaker returning with two fat parcels in his cart. Frod had seen them too and stood hopping from one foot to the other in his excitement.

The cart stopped and in a flash Frod was pulling off his old boots. They unwrapped the parcels and watched as the round giant pulled on his brand new blue boots. Everyone gasped the boots had WINGS.

The bouncy giant stood up and the wings on his heels carried him forwards.

Yes, his boots could fly!

'Hwittuc, dear Hwittuc throw down the key.
My boots are fantastic, come here and see.'

But no one appeared. They heard an enormous sneeze like thunder. Hwittuc had a bad cold. He was dressed in his woolly hat with a blanket round his shoulders.

'Stand still Frod, I will throw the key to your feet,'and he sneezed again.

They all saw the flash of the key in the sunlight and heard a squawk from a passing bird but no one saw the key land.

'Hwittuc where is the key?
It's not here, where can it be?'

Poor Hwittuc blew his nose hard and wiped a tear from his eye. He had seen that thieving jackdaw fly down and snatch the key out of the air. Worse still, as the bird flew off he squawked and the key fell out of his beak straight into the moat.

Sam, Dotty and Lawley had seen this, so had the shoemaker and his boy. Everyone was upset. Frod cried out,

'Our key is too heavy, it cannot float.
It's lost for ever, in Stokesay moat.'

Then he wailed louder and louder. How could he pay the shoemaker for these magical boots? All his money was locked up in the chest behind the cellar door... and the key was in the moat.

The shoemaker suggested that if Frod felt able to give him his hen with the golden feather that would be enough payment. The giant agreed and in no time at all he flew home and returned with the hen clutched tightly under his arm.

'Feed her well, she's the best hen ever,
Eggs every day, whatever the weather.'

So the shoemaker went home happy. The two giants agreed to meet again tomorrow to search for the key.

Blink, Blink... the next morning arrived. Both giants, dressed in old clothes and waterproof boots were standing by the castle moat. Tall Hwittuc stepped into the moat and began scooping out buckets of muddy water. Frod stayed on the bank and sifted through each bucketful. He was happy. He loved water and mud.

Hours went by but no key was found. How Sam longed to help them, but he could only watch. He saw Frod throwing snails, fish and newts back into the water while Hwittuc collected the rusty tins and nails and broken pots.

'This is no use Frod, the key may lie hidden for ever. We must forget our treasure chest deep in the cellar. We will save all the rent from our farms and we grow our own food, we can manage. And our new boots will last for years and years.'

'Come,' whispered Lawley. He made Sam jump.

'We must be gone, the magic is almost done.' He flicked his tail round them both and sat them on his back. 'Eyes shut tight and hold on.'

In no time at all they were sitting on the stones at the top of the orchard. Lawley could tell that Sam was worrying about the key.

'Listen Sam, Frod and Hwittuc are hardworking giants, they will be fine.'

'But the key, the treasure chest, what will happen now?'

'All I know Sam, is that Granpa Doc has ordered the dragons on Stokesay Castle gatehouse to keep watch. If they see anyone with that key those dragons will call him. Granpa Doc will use his strongest magic. All will be well.'

'In days to come, it is foretold'
That mighty key, it will be found.
'Midst ash keys hung in branches old
Or midst *cowslip bells upon the ground.
(*cowslip flowers are called St Peter's Keys)

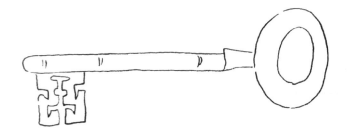

Whoosh! Lawley was gone, leaving Sam with his head full of questions.

Could *he* solve the mystery?

A voice woke him from his daydreaming. It was Gran calling him in for lunch.

# *MAP*

Use this map and discover places that Lawley visited. Have an adventure of your own.

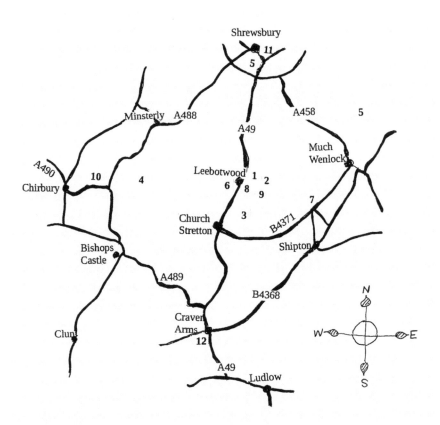

1. **Lawley** - 'The Lawley' Walk on his back, it's a long way to his tail.

2. **Flying Flags** - Kites fly well from Lawley's back.

3 **Granpa Caradoc** - 'Caer Caradoc', this is where Granpa Doc lives. Lawley is to the North.

4. **Dragon Magic at Stiperstones** - Park at the 'Knolls Car Park' in the Stiperstones National Nature Reserve and take a walk to look for the stone where Lawley took Sam to meet Wild Edric. Visit 'The Bog Visitor Centre' for refreshments.

5.i **Shrewsbury Shoemaker** -In the Dingle Gardens at the 'Quarry Park' in Shrewsbury, find the 'Shoemakers Arbour' by the pool, Bodkin may have collected his shoes here?

5.ii The giant's spadeful of earth made the huge hill 'The Wrekin', north of Much Wenlock. You can park at the bottom of the Wrekin to walk up to the very top. If you would like to see the giant you can visit him in 'Telford Town Park'.

6 **Harvest at Leebotwood** - Go inside 'St. Mary Church' and look for two carved dragons up near the roof.

7 **Sh... Ippikin will catch you** - Ippikin's Rock lies adjacent to B4371 on 'Wenlock Edge'

8 **Gran's Secret** - Look out for a trilobite fossil stone like Gran's in the Ludlow or Shrewsbury museum.

9 **Where are the Matches?** - Lawley flew over his hill on bonfire night.

10 **Mitchell the Witch** - Look out for the sign to Mitchell's fold, walk up to the stone circle and find the tallest stone.

11 **Mischief in Shrewsbury** - Along the Mardol in Shrewsbury town centre, find the upside down dragon who hangs from a beam on the corner of a shop. He looks as mischievous as Lawley.

12 **Stokesay Giants' Treasure** - See the dragons carved on the Gatehouse and find the North Tower of 'Stokesay Castle' where the giant's treasure chest lies hidden. Walk along the moat. Can you see any Ash Keys or Cowslips?

#0019 - 091118 - C0 - 203/133/6 - PB - 9781912419425